Bee
Love
(Can Be Hard)

Bee
Love
(Can Be Hard)

by Alan Page and Kamie Page

illustrated by David Geister

PAGE EDUCATION FOUNDATION
MINNEAPOLIS, MINNESOTA

Thump... Thump... Thump...

The soccer ball bounced back to Otis' feet in a perfect rhythm.

Thump... Thump... Thump...

Otis was so focused on the beat of the ball he didn't notice the soft, velvety hum of danger floating in the air. He was just about to head inside for some water when he heard it.

Buzzzzzzzzzz...

Otis panicked. Arms flailing, he raced to the back door.

"Help! Grandpa! Bee attack! Open the door!"

Otis wasn't scared of many things, but at the top of his list? Bees.

"Bee attack! Grandpa! Open the door!"

"Otis! What on earth…"

"Grandpa! Bees! They're gonna get me!"

Otis' grandpa held him in a hug. "No, Otis, they're not going to get you."

"But Grandpa," Otis insisted, "they're out there!"

"You're okay, kiddo," Grandpa said. "Try and take some deep breaths."

But Otis couldn't breathe. He closed his eyes tight and pinched his body shut.

"Otis, bees are out there, and being stung by a bee is no laughing matter, but bees are probably more frightened of you than you are of them."

Otis looked up. He'd heard all of this before. Disbelief wrinkled his eyebrows.

"It's true!" Grandpa said. "A bee stings to protect its hive. Once it stings, it dies, so it has no interest in—"

"Grandpa," Otis interrupted, "how do you know so much about bees?"

"When I was your age, I had a healthy fear of bees," Grandpa explained.

"You did?"

"I did! And I wasn't alone. My friend Jerry and I were so afraid we started a club to get rid of all the bees in our neighborhood."

"You mean your friend Farmer Jerry?"

"Yep, Farmer Jerry. Back then we didn't understand bees. They just seemed scary. Fortunately, we weren't successful. As it turns out, bees are amazing insects. They're pollinating powerhouses! So much of what we eat is a direct result of their hard work."

Otis' face scrunched.

"In fact, Jerry doesn't run just any farm, he runs a bee farm!"

That did it. *A bee farm?* Otis knew his fun-loving Grandpa was pulling his leg.

"It's true! The farm even has a Learning Lab. Sometimes, learning about what you're afraid of is the best way to face it. That way, it's not so mysterious and scary. I think it's time we paid Farmer Jerry a visit."

Otis wasn't so sure. That night, a swarm of bees attacked his dreams. Supersized stingers surrounded his bed. They were about to get him when . . .

...Buzzzzzzzzzz...
Buzzzzzzzzzz...

Heart racing, Otis' eyes popped open. *Nope!* He said to himself. *I am not going to any bee farm, and I am not going to have anything else to do with bees.*

ING CENTER

A frown followed Otis all the way to the farm. But when he got out of the car, Farmer Jerry greeted him with a wide grin. "Welcome to Lily Haven Bee Farm!"

Even though Otis could feel Jerry's warmth, a cold chill crept up his legs as he tried to muster the courage to move his feet forward.

"Where are the cows and pigs?" Otis mumbled. "Isn't this a farm?"

"Oh sure, it's a farm, all right. It's a farm for flowers and bees. We've got a few chickens and goats roaming around here somewhere, but we mostly focus on pollinators, like honeybees. Without pollination from wind and insects, there would be no seeds, no fruits, no vegetables. Can you imagine? I believe it's our job to help protect all bees and keep them safe."

Otis found it hard to concentrate. *Protect them! What about protecting me?* Bees seemed to be everywhere, taunting him, buzzing out a warning, telling him to stay away. He scooched closer to Grandpa.

"Visitors are often worried about being here," Jerry went on. "It's normal. No one wants to get stung. Bee love *can* be hard."

"I remember when your grandpa and I wouldn't dare go in the backyard, let alone to a bee farm! Let's get your beekeeping gear on. It'll help you feel more protected."

Otis gave Jerry a doubtful sideways glance. Noticing Otis' hesitation, Jerry bent down to look Otis in the eyes. "Just remember, stay calm and breathe. Try taking a few slow, mindful breaths and repeat the words: 'The bees do not want to sting me'."

Heading to the meadow, Otis paid close attention to the bees and his breathing. *The bees do not want to sting me. The bees do not want to sting me. The bees do not want to sting me.*

As the bees floated on the gentle breeze, dipping in and out of flowers, Otis noticed his body relaxing. Unexpectedly, he also realized the bees weren't taunting him—they were simply beautiful.

"If you look closely, you can see balls of pollen gathering on their hind legs," Jerry said.

Otis was curious, but he still didn't want to get too close. He took a deep breath in, let a deep breath out, and then bent down. "Wow," he marveled.

The wooden hives were electric with activity. The bees were busy. Jerry was busy too. While he prepared to open a hive by using a bee smoker to calm the bees, he explained that all 50,000 bees in the hive had different jobs—protecting the hive, cleaning, gathering pollen, feeding nectar to the young, making honey . . .

Otis liked the sound of honey, but the number 50,000 made him want to faint. *Fifty-thousand bees in each hive?*

Jerry pulled out a frame covered with bees. It was filled with honeycomb and dripping with honey. "If you're lucky, you may catch a glimpse of the queen. A sharp eye can spot her larger body, but there's only one in there, so …"

Deep breath in, deep breath out. The bees do not want to sting me. As if in a trance, Otis watched the busy bees buzz and dance and work.

Jerry asked if Otis wanted to hold the frame. Otis was calm like the bees, but his hands shook slightly as he surprised himself and nodded. The bees ignored him as he took hold. He almost didn't hear Jerry whisper, "There she is!"

The queen. Otis couldn't believe it. With each breath in, his fear breathed out. "Amazing!" he whispered back.

Back at the Learning Lab, Jerry took time to answer Otis' many questions about bees . . .

It's true! Ninety-nine percent of all honeybees you see are female!

about beekeeping . . .

If you respect the bees, they will respect you.

and about honey . . .

Yes, honey is really basically bee barf.

Otis and Grandpa giggled as they tried several sweet samples.

The frown that followed Otis to the farm that morning had been replaced, just like his fears. Smiling, he asked, "Grandpa, can we come back?"

Grandpa and Farmer Jerry shared a smile. "Anytime," Jerry offered.

While Otis still didn't want to be stung, he now knew that bees didn't have any interest in stinging him. They had other, more important jobs to do, and so did he.

The Buzz About Bees

Bees are important insects. They come in different colors, shapes, and sizes. While their bodies are small, they are also fascinating! They have one long tongue, two stomachs, three body parts (head, thorax, and abdomen), four wings, five eyes, six legs, and millions of tiny hairs.

There are over 20,000 different bee species in the world and around 3,000 in the United States! Honeybees, bumblebees, and mason bees are just a few of the bees you might see flying around your neighborhood.

While honeybees are not native to North America, they, like other native bees, are pollinators. This means they help flowers, plants, trees, fruits, and vegetables grow.

Within a honeybee hive, there are three different types of adult bees—drones, workers, and the queen. The drones are the males. They are the fattest of the three, and their job is to mate with a queen (the longest) so she can lay up to 2,000 eggs a day. The workers are all female, and they are the smallest, both in width and length. The workers have a lot of jobs. To name a few, they keep the hive clean and protect it, they take care of the young bees inside the hive, they gather nectar for food, pollinate flowers, and make beeswax, which is used to help build the hive and store honey.

Beehives are often found underground, in hollow tree trunks, hanging on tree branches, or in places where they aren't likely to be disturbed. Honeybee nests are made of honeycomb. Honeycomb is beeswax that has been built into small hexagon-shaped cells.

Beekeepers, or apiarists, often use bee boxes to mimic a wild beehive. They often wear protective bee suits and use smoke to confuse, but also calm, the bees. This helps keep beekeepers safe. If you would like more information on bees, beekeeping, or how you can help protect these little pollinating powerhouses, please head to www.PollinateMN.org, or look up your local beekeeping advocates.

PAGE EDUCATION FOUNDATION

CREATING HEROES THROUGH EDUCATION AND SERVICE

The Page Education Foundation, started by Alan and Diane Page in 1988, assists Minnesota young people of color in two ways: Page Scholars receive financial assistance for their post-secondary education, and in turn volunteer at least fifty hours each year working with schoolchildren as real-life role models for success. Students at all levels of academic achievement qualify to become a Page Scholar, a distinction that is awarded based on an applicant's educational goals, willingness to volunteer with children, and financial need. Every student has potential, but many need support to realize their dreams.

All proceeds from the sale of this book support the Page Education Foundation. To learn more about the Foundation and to order copies of the book, visit www.page-ed.org.

To the love of my life, Diane Sims Page, forever and always, my honeybee.
—A. P.

To my mom, Diane Sims Page. All of the flowers in this book are for you.
—K. P.

To my grandchildren—you make the world look so beautiful.
—D. G.

Acknowledgments

We are grateful to Garrick, the model who brought our main character to life,
Jerry Blackwell, a.k.a. Farmer Jerry, of Peacehaven Farm, Jordan, Minnesota, for welcoming us
and sharing his passion for beekeeping, and Erin Rupp at Pollinate Minnesota for educating
us, and advocating for all things "bee." We could not have made this book without you.

Text copyright © 2020 Alan Page and Kamie Page
Illustrations copyright © 2020 Book Bridge Press
Illustrations by David Geister
Design by Joe Fahey

Page Education Foundation
P.O. Box 581254
Minneapolis, MN 55458
www.page-ed.org
info@page-ed.org

Printed and bound in the United States of America

First Edition
LCCN 2020908133
ISBN 978-0-578-68975-3

This book was expertly produced by Book Bridge Press.

www.bookbridgepress.com